For my Dad, who taught me how to draw,
and let me stay up late to watch comedy

And for my Mum, who has bought loads of copies
and given them as gifts to friends and family
despite not getting a good 90% of the jokes.

I love you lots.

To
Anne
& Rob

Thanks
P.

GW00707383

4

5

7

IN BRITAIN, THE
COOKIE MONSTER
IS KNOWN AS

BISCUIT ABOMINATION

9

12

13

JOHN VIRGO: SNOOKER COMMENTATOR

14

DIVORCED

BEHEADED

DIED

DIVORCED

BEHEADED

SURVIVED

16

THIS IS WHY NASA EMPLOYEES AREN'T ALLOWED TO DATE THE ASTRONAUTS

I've been working on
a cocktail called

Grounds for Divorce

It's a Piña Colada
I've pissed in

THIS WINE IS A FULL BODIED WHITE, DRY WITH NOTES OF APPLES

PINOT BLANC

THIS WINE IS LIGHT BODIED AND SWEET, WITH A PEPPERY, ALMOST ACIDIC FINISH

PINOT GRIGIO

THIS WINE HITS LIKE A .38 SLUG, LINGERS LIKE A DAME'S PERFUME, FINISHES LIKE A HAMMER TO THE SKULL

PINOT NOIR

I HOPED THERE WOULD BE NO RAMIFICATIONS FROM BUYING A SOFA...

...FROM DEATH...

BUT, THERE WERE SOME UNFORTUNATE REAPER CUSHIONS

24

THE HIDDEN MEANING OF EQUESTRIAN STATUES

27

28

MY WORST NIGHTMARE

NEVER
SAY DIE

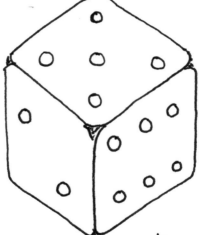

I KNOW IT'S
SINGULAR FOR
DICE, BUT IT JUST
SOUNDS STUPID

THE EASIEST WAY TO FOIL JAMES BOND

IS TO BE AN INCREDIBLY ATTRACTIVE WOMAN WITH A NORMAL NAME

MR BOND? SARAH COOPER. DON'T BOTHER, I'VE HEARD ALL THE JOKES

HE WILL GET STUCK TRYING TO MAKE A PUN.

COOP 'ER? I BARELY KNOW 'ER! Nooo... YOU COULD HAVE ME OVER A BARREL - NOPE. SOMETHING ABOUT CHURNS?

WHILST YOU GET ON WITH YOUR NEFARIOUS SCHEME.

DOOMSDAY DEVICE MK 4

...WHERE YOU SEE ONE SET OF FOOTPRINTS, THAT, MY SON, IS WHERE I CARRIED YOU

JESUS, WHAT ABOUT THESE HANDPRINTS

THAT, MY SON, IS WHERE I DID SOMETHING PREEEEEEETTY COOL!

MEANWHILE, AT THE HEADQUARTERS OF THE JUSTICE LEAGUE

39

40

WOMEN WHO USE BREASTMILK PUMPS
YOU GO GIRLS!
KEEP EXPRESSING YOURSELVES!

SCARE YOUR FRIENDS

WITH A JIMMY HILL-O-WEEN MASK!

THE DIFFERENCE BETWEEN KNOWLEDGE AND WISDOM

KNOWLEDGE: KNOWING THAT 'GYMNASIUM' IS GREEK FOR "EXERCISE NAKED"

WISDOM: THE KNOWLEDGE THAT DOING SO WILL GET YOU BANNED FROM EVERY FITNESS FIRST IN THE COUNTRY

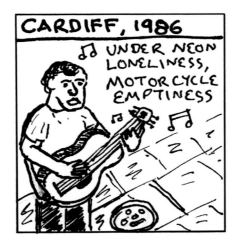

MICHAEL STIPE'S HOLIDAY PHOTOS

48

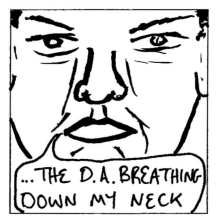

50

51

YOU KNOW WHAT REALLY BOILS MY PISS?
PISSBOT 5000
CAN'T RECOMMEND IT ENOUGH
FIVE STARS

WHEN THE WEATHER GETS LIKE THIS

THERE'S NOTHING BETTER THAN MAKING A ROARING FIRE

THEN USING IT TO FORGE WEAPONS OF UNIMAGINABLE POWER

HOBOCOP

PART MAN, PART TRAMP, ALL COP

MRS HENDERON? I'M AFRAID I HAVE SOME BAD NEWS. A BODY WASHED UP ON THE BANKS OF THE RIVER

OH GOOD LORD

WE'LL NEED YOU TO COME AND IDENTIFY IT, AS IT MATCHES THE DESCRIPTION OF JASON. THERE'S JUST ONE THING ELSE I NEED...

SOB WHAT?

I NEED TEN PENCE FOR A CUP OF TEA

AARGH! GET AWAY FROM ME, YOU BEASTLY VAGRANT

55

Sesame Street is set in Queens, New York.
If it was set in the Bronx, it would be more like

CAUGHT BY THE CHILD SOLDIERS...

...OF COLOMBIA'S MOST NOTORIOUS DRUG CARTEL...

DO YOU HAVE ANY FINAL WORDS?

I'D HAVE GOT AWAY WITH IT...

...IF IT WASN'T FOR YOU MEDELLÍN KIDS!

NEW TV SHOW IDEA: DAVID FROST TAKES ALL THE KETAMINE

LLOYD GROSSMAN HAS TO TALK HIM THROUGH IT.

THAT'S *Through* the K-Hole

66

LOW SHELF ESTEEM

DUE TO RISING OBESITY RATES
GRAVES ARE BEING DUG WIDER

THE PLOT THICKENS

GRANGE HILL

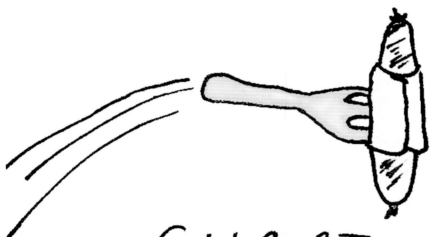

CHRISTMAS SPECIAL

WHAT'S DOPAMINE

IS DOPAYOURS

74

THE INTERNET: LOVES PICTURES OF CUTE CATS...

...LOVES PICTURES OF COMPLICATED MEALS...

YET, WHEN I MADE "KITTEN TIKKA MASSALA"...

RSPCA! OPEN UP!

THE CLUB CAN'T EVEN HANDLE ME RIGHT NOW

I'VE LOST MY CLOAKROOM STUB

AND I'M HOLDING UP THE QUEUE.

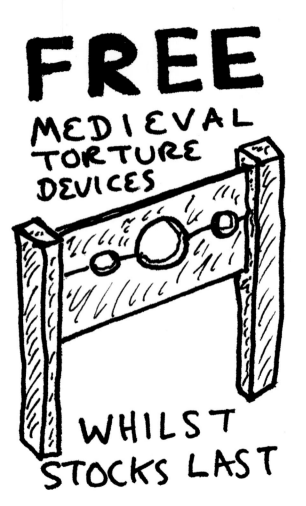

LEARN TRIGONOMETRY THROUGH CLASSIC NOIR CINEMA...

WITH "HERE'S LOOKING AT EUCLID"

DUE TO A CLERICAL ERROR IN REALITY, THIS WEEKEND I WENT ROCK CLIMBING IN A NOTIONAL PARK

81

ABOUT THE ARTIST

Paul Savage was born in Liverpool in 1984, and grew up in Wolverhampton. Before starting comedy, he was variously a youth worker, used car salesman and call centre worker, and about 40 other things he got fired from.

After starting to do comedy in 2007, he has written and performed 7 solo shows at the Edinburgh Fringe Festival, co-wrote and starred in the critically acclaimed game show Hell To Play, and performed sell out shows at The Adelaide Fringe and Melbourne International Comedy Festival.

In 2017 he was was featured in the 'Top 10 Jokes of the Edinburgh Fringe' lists in The Guardian, The Mirror, Esquire, Shortlist and The Week.

This is his third book of comic strips, although 95% of the first two are included in this book.

He lives in London and has built a cocktail bar in his living room so everything is going great, thanks.

ABOUT THE PUBLISHER

McKnight & Bishop are always on the lookout for great new authors and ideas for exciting new books. If you write or if you have an idea for a book, email us: info@mcknightbishop.com

Some things we love are: undiscovered authors, open-source software, crowdfunding, Amazon/Kindle, social networking, faith, laughter and new ideas.

Visit us at www.mcknightbishop.com

ABOUT PERIL DESIGN

Peril Design is Paul Banks. He mostly designs artwork for comedy shows, tours and festivals. He didn't design this book, but he did update it and prepare the new version for print.

CREDITS

Thanks goes to, for having an idea and letting me redraw it:

- Joz Norris for 'New York as a Character'
- Matt Green for 'Little Boys Room'
- Danny Sutcliffe for 'Grounds For Divorce'
- Andy Kind for 'Table for 4'
- The Teenage Workshop at 'Comedy Club 4 Kids', who I taught comics to, and one scampish *then-11-year-old* Kieran Boulton who drew 'There's A Girl In My Class', which I've redrawn with his permission.